For Lindsey, with love and thanks — LR
For Lily, Florence, and Albie with love from Marg —MC

First published in the United Kingdom in 2008 by Chicken House, 2 Palmer Street, Frome, Somerset BA11 1DS.

ISBN: 978-0-545-22617-2

12 11 10 9 8 7 6 5 4 3 2 1   10 11 12 13 14 15/0

Printed in the U.S.A.   08

First Scholastic paperback printing, January 2010

Text was set in P22DaddyO-Hip.

Book design by Ian Butterworth

Pink!

by Lynne Rickards
illustrated by Margaret Chamberlain

SCHOLASTIC INC.
New York Toronto London Auckland
Sydney Mexico City New Delhi Hong Kong

One sunny morning, Patrick woke up to find he had turned bright

Pink!

His beak was pink, his flippers were pink — he was pink from head to foot

"This is terrible!" cried Patrick.

"What will all my friends say? Whoever heard of a pink penguin?"

"Don't worry, dear," soothed his mom,
"Dr. Black will soon sort you out."

Dr. Black was puzzled.
She looked in her
big medical book.

ABCs of
HEALTH

"A very cold penguin can turn BLUE," she said. "If you're feeling queasy you can go a bit GREEN.

But PINK is very unusual."

Dr. Black closed her big book. "Perhaps you'll get used to being pink . . . ," she said to Patrick.

"But I'm a BOY!" he shouted. "And BOYS CAN'T BE PINK!"

When they got home, Patrick's dad opened another big book. It was called

BIRDS of the WORLD.

"Look," he said to Patrick, "flamingos are pink, just like you."

Patrick looked. He saw hundreds of beautiful birds.

"Are some of them boys?" asked Patrick as he gazed at the picture.

"At least half of them," laughed his dad. "You see, boys can be pink."

Patrick got teased at school for being pink.
"Don't worry, they'll get used to it soon enough," said his mom.

Patrick wasn't so sure.
He didn't like being different from everyone else.

One Saturday morning, Patrick pulled out his backpack. He put in his pajamas and his favorite plush toy.

"I don't fit in here anymore," he told his mom and dad. "I'm going to Africa to see those flamingos."

Patrick went to the water's edge. Africa was a long way north, but he was a strong swimmer. He swam for seven days and seven nights.

When the water began to feel warmer, he knew he was nearly there.

On the eighth day, Patrick arrived in a wide bay. On the shore he saw hundreds of flamingos, just like in the picture! He waddled up to them and held out a pink flipper. "How do you do?" he said politely.

The flamingos looked down at him curiously. They had long necks and spindly legs and were very, very tall. "Will you join us for lunch?" one of them asked Patrick. "Oh, yes, thank you!" he cried.

All the flamingos dipped their long, curvy beaks in the water and began skimming them back and forth. Patrick's beak was quite the wrong shape, so he came up coughing and spluttering. Poor Patrick would have to go hungry!

After lunch, the flamingos took a nap.
They all stood on one leg and tucked their heads down.
Patrick tried to stand on one leg, too. He was hopeless!

When sunset came, it was time to fly to the nesting ground. The flamingos flapped their wings and rose into the air like a big pink cloud.

One small pink penguin was left behind.

"This is no good," said Patrick. He didn't belong here, even though he was pink. It was time to go home.

The next morning, Patrick set off. He swam for seven days and seven nights, until the water felt lovely and cold again.

When Patrick went back to school, his whole class crowded around him. "Where have you been, Patrick?" they asked. "We missed you!"

Patrick's mom and dad were very pleased to see him.

"You must have missed your favorite breakfast," said Dad.

"I sure did!" said Patrick with his mouth full.

Patrick's teacher asked him to give a little talk about his travels. He stood at the front of the class with a big map and a pointer.

"I went to Africa," Patrick told his friends.

"Wow, you swam all that way?" asked Billy.

Patrick nodded proudly.

"In Africa the water is warm," he continued. "There are colorful fish and tall pink birds called flamingos that stand on one leg."

"Did you see one of those?" asked Lulu.

"I saw hundreds!" answered Patrick. "They were beautiful. But, you know, they can't swim underwater or slide on their tummies like we can."

"Really?" said his classmates.
"What a shame!"

After school, Patrick waddled home with his best friend, Arthur.
"You know, Arthur," said Patrick, "I'm really glad I went to Africa."
"I'm really glad you came back!" said Arthur.

"Me, too!"
laughed Patrick.

"Penguins belong at the South Pole.
Even pink penguins."

"Especially pink penguins!" said Arthur happily.

That night at bedtime, Patrick said,

"You were right, Mom.
Nobody teases me anymore."

He snuggled down and smiled.
Being different wasn't so bad after all.